About This Book

Darkness at Noon is an important book on several counts. When it appeared in 1941 it shed light on the Moscow treason trials and the abject confessions incredible to the Western mind. Today its reading is even more imperative for those who would understand the Communist emphasis on Ends Rather Than Means. A short book, it is a miracle of compression: it conveys in dramatic form the essence of all political philosophy and the basic differences between two warring attitudes: to one of which the individual is of supreme importance as to the other he is supremely unimportant.

However to suggest that it is a didactic novel like *Uncle Tom's Cabin* would be entirely misleading. Although it is a portrait of a nation and a way of life, it is chiefly the portrait of an individual. Like all great novelists, Koestler has made his protagonist, the Old Bolshevik Rubashov, stand for all mankind and in his death we are all involved. Nowhere is the moral stressed, nowhere are deductions drawn by the author. There are no asides. Irony alone provides the key. The moral conflict unfolds dramatically in the thoughts and recollections of its hero, in his cross-examination at the hands of police magistrates and his relationships with his fellow-prisoners—particularly in his conversations tapped through the cell wall with a White Russian, a type whom he cannot help despising. Worn-out, disillusioned (more actively involved than the Old Bolshevik in Mark Aldanov's *The Fifth Seal*), Rubashov sloughs off years of disciplined thinking to arrive at an appreciation of what he has learnt to call the "gramm[ar of] fiction," the "I" who is more than a ciph[er in an eco]nomic scheme. Here is one of the cla[ssics], [the] story of crime an[d punishment in its] varying [...]

'He who establishes a dictatorship and does not kill Brutus, or he who founds a republic and does not kill the sons of Brutus, will only reign a short time.'

MACHIAVELLI:
Discorsi

'Man, man, one cannot live quite without pity.'
DOSTOEVSKY:
Crime and Punishment